# THE WORLD SERIES

by Jeff Hawkins

Published by ABDO Publishing Company, PO Box 398166, Minneapolis, MN 55439. Copyright © 2013 by Abdo Consulting Group, Inc. International copyrights reserved in all countries. No part of this book may be reproduced in any form without written permission from the publisher. SportsZone™ is a trademark and logo of ABDO Publishing Company.

Printed in the United States of America,
North Mankato, Minnesota
112012
012013

 THIS BOOK CONTAINS AT LEAST 10% RECYCLED MATERIALS.

Editor: Chrös McDougall
Series Designer: Craig Hinton

**Photo Credits:** Sue Ogrocki/AP Images, cover; Hans Deryk/AP Images, title; Jeff Roberson/AP Images, 5; Eric Gay/AP Images, 9; Matt Slocum/AP Images, 11; AP Images, 13, 19, 21, 27, 31, 58 (top, left and right), 60 (bottom, left); Omikron Omikron/Getty Images, 15; Mark Rucker/Transcendental Graphics/Getty Images, 24, 59 (top); Focus On Sport/Getty Images, 33; Harry Cabluck/AP Images, 37, 58 (bottom); Dick Raphael/Sports Illustrated/Getty Images, 39; Stan Grossfeld/The Boston Globe/Getty Images, 41; Getty Images, 44; Jim Mone/AP Images, 48, 59 (bottom, left); Mark Lennihanl/AP Images, 51; Amy Sancetta/AP Images, 55, 59 (bottom, right); David J. Phillip/AP Images, 57; Tiffany and Co./AP Images, 60 (top); Susan Walsh/AP Images, 60 (bottom, right)

**Cataloging-in-Publication Data**
Hawkins, Jeff.
 The World Series / Jeff Hawkins.
   p. cm. -- (Sports' great championships)
Includes bibliographical references and index.
ISBN 978-1-61783-676-3
1. Baseball--History--Juvenile literature.  2. World Series (Baseball)--History--Juvenile literature.  I. Title.
796.357/646--dc22

                                    2012946236

# TABLE OF CONTENTS

# A Modern Classic

It was the final brush stroke of a World Series Game 6 masterpiece. David Freese, the St. Louis Cardinals' third baseman, stepped up to the plate against Texas Rangers pitcher Mark Lowe. The sold-out Busch Stadium crowd turned its collective attention to the pitch.

*BOOM!*

With one powerful swing, Freese sent the ball 429 feet (130.8 m) and over the center field wall. And when the ball landed in the grassy knoll beyond the fence, it capped off one of the most remarkable games in

St. Louis Cardinals third baseman David Freese runs around the bases after hitting his 11th-inning, game-winning home run in Game 6 of the 2011 World Series.

World Series history. The 11th-inning, walk-off home run on October 27, 2011, gave St. Louis a 10–9 come-from-behind victory and ended the marathon, 4-hour, 33-minute game. The win kept the Cardinals alive for Game 7.

Freese's Cardinals teammates waited at home plate as he completed his home-run trot. When he arrived, they literally ripped apart his jersey. It was a breathless journey for Freese and the Cardinals. Their World Series campaign had been on the brink just minutes earlier.

## Ninth-Inning Comeback

It was the bottom of the ninth inning. The Rangers led the series three games to two. They came into the final half-inning with a 7–5 lead. Then they recorded two outs. Most of the 47,325 fans at Busch Stadium were wearing Cardinals red and waving white towels. First baseman Albert Pujols and outfielder Lance Berkman were on base. The Cardinals needed a hero. That is when Freese stepped to the plate.

On the mound, however, was Rangers star closer Neftali Feliz. Freese had never faced Feliz. "Initially, I was like: 'Are you kidding me? My first [at-bat] off Feliz in this situation,'" Freese joked after the game.

Feliz quickly had his opponent down to his final strike. But on the next pitch, Freese connected. The ball sailed over the head of Rangers right fielder Nelson Cruz. Late in close games, outfielders generally play deeper

## Powerful Pujols

No player produced as much power in a World Series game as Cardinals first baseman Albert Pujols did in Game 3 in 2011. Pujols established a record with 14 total bases. He also tied single-game records for hits (five), home runs (three), and runs batted in (RBIs) (six). And he scored four runs in the Cardinals' win. Only the New York Yankees' Babe Ruth in 1926 and 1928 and Reggie Jackson in 1977 had hit three homers in a single World Series game. The San Francisco Giants' Pablo Sandoval matched that feat in 2012. Pujols's five hits equaled a record set by the Milwaukee Brewers' Paul Molitor in 1982. His six RBIs also tied two Yankees (Bobby Richardson in 1960 and Hideki Matsui in 2009).

to prevent extra-base hits. But Cruz was stationed shallow and could not catch up to the long liner.

"I just beared down, got a pitch to hit," Freese explained. "Initially, I thought I hit it pretty good. I thought [Cruz] was going to grab it." But Cruz could not. Freese reached third base safely for a triple. Pujols and Berkman scored with ease, tying the game at 7–7. The game moved into extra innings. "A lot of emotions on that one," Freese said.

## The Victory

Cardinals closer Jason Motte returned to the mound for the top of the 10th inning. He got the first batter out. Then he gave up a single

## A Hometown Hero

David Freese was not always a World Series hero. There was a time when he had to work extra hard to overcome injuries and become a special player. In 2009, Freese approached superstar teammate Albert Pujols for extra assistance. Pujols invited Freese to his offseason workouts.

Freese watched, listened, and learned from the future Hall of Famer. When it was his turn to practice, Freese did so with everything he had. "Every swing he took, I could learn something," Freese said of Pujols. Freese learned his lessons well. In Game 6 of the 2011 World Series, he slugged a walk-off home run. It was only the 15th walk-off home run in World Series history.

For Freese, his World Series success story truly is a childhood dream come true. He grew up in Wildwood, Missouri. It is approximately 45 minutes from Busch Stadium in downtown St. Louis. Freese grew up cheering for the Cardinals.

to center field. To the plate stepped Rangers center fielder Josh Hamilton. He had been the American League (AL) Most Valuable Player (MVP) in 2010. He showed why in this at-bat. Hamilton launched a two-run homer off Motte's blazing 98-mph pitch. Just like that, the Rangers were again up by two runs, 9–7.

Once again, the Cardinals' season was on the brink in the bottom of the inning. And they would have to rely on the bottom of their batting order to start a rally. The Cardinals opened the inning with two singles. A sacrifice bunt advanced the runners. Second baseman Ryan Theriot's groundout scored a run.

St. Louis Cardinals players wait for third baseman David Freese to touch home and end the marathon Game 6 of the 2011 World Series.

Pujols, the Cardinals' most dangerous slugger, was up next. The Rangers intentionally walked him.

With two outs and runners on first and second, Berkman stepped to the plate. Now it was his turn to be the hero. The veteran outfielder hit a single to center that scored a run and tied the game again at 9–9. It was his third hit and third RBI of the game.

After holding the Rangers scoreless in the top of the 11th, Freese hit the game-winning homer in the bottom of the inning. Capping the comeback, the Cardinals became the first team in 107 World Series to rally from 9th- and 10th-inning deficits. They were also the first to score in the 8th, 9th, 10th, and 11th innings. Said Cardinals manager Tony La Russa: "You had to be here to believe it."

## Cards Second Only to Yanks

The 2011 World Series championship was the Cardinals' eleventh. Only the New York Yankees had more. Through 2012, the Yankees had captured the most World Series titles (27) and made the most appearances (40). The Giants were next with 19 appearances and seven wins. St. Louis had 18 appearances and 11 wins.

## The Series Finale

The World Series went to a decisive Game 7 for the first time since 2002. For the Cardinals, it turned out to be a nine-inning celebration in front of the home fans at Busch Stadium.

Freese confirmed his candidacy for World Series MVP early in Game 7. Rangers starting pitcher Matt Harrison walked consecutive batters, Pujols and Berkman. Freese was up next. He battled to a full count. Both base runners were running with the pitch. And both scored easily on Freese's hit to right-center field. Freese's spark propelled the Cardinals to a 6–2 victory and secured the team's eleventh World Series title.

"This whole ride, this team deserves this," said Freese, who was named MVP of the National League (NL) Championship Series (NLCS) and the World Series. "This is definitely a dream come true."

St. Louis Cardinals catcher Yadier Molina reacts after the final out in Game 7 of the 2011 World Series as his teammates pour onto the field to celebrate the victory.

It was an improbable championship run for the Cardinals. On August 25, they were 10 1/2 games behind in the wild-card race. But they rallied. St. Louis qualified for the postseason on the last game of the regular season and marched into history.

Freese was an important part. His 21 postseason RBIs established a new record. His performance earned praise from his teammates.

"He's got 'it'" Berkman said. "I don't know what 'it' is, but he's got it. He's one of those players that can perform when it matters the most. The moment is never bigger than he is."

Since 1903, fans have gotten used to those kinds of heroics at the Fall Classic.

# Chapter 2

# Chasing Pennants

**B**aseball's true origin remains a mystery. The sport could date back to 1791, possibly further. But the first reference to the game was that year in Pittsfield, Massachusetts. A city ordinance banned the game from being played within 80 yards of the town meeting hall.

Officially, most people recognize Abner Doubleday as baseball's founder. Doubleday supposedly formed most of the game's rules in 1839. However, baseball scholars have long disputed the claim. Over the centuries, people played several games involving a bat, a ball, and

Though baseball's origins are disputed, Union General Abner Doubleday is officially credited with inventing the sport in 1839 in Cooperstown, New York.

## The "$30,000 Muff"

The 1912 World Series featured the New York Giants and the Boston Red Sox. In the 10th inning of the decisive Game 8, a routine fly ball was hit toward Giants center fielder Fred Snodgrass. But he dropped it. The fumble allowed the Red Sox to steal the title in dramatic fashion. Four games in the highly charged series were decided by only one run. One game was called due to darkness, forcing Game 8. Snodgrass's miscue became known as the "$30,000 muff." That is because the winning team received $30,000 more than the losing team.

running. Early forms of baseball went by "goal ball," "fletch-catch," "stool ball," and "base." A few of those pastimes, such as cricket and rounders, are still played today.

Doubleday was a combat-tested Civil War officer. In his lifetime, he never claimed to be the founder of baseball. The Doubleday legend grew beginning in 1907. A group called the Mills Commission was put together to determine the game's origin. It concluded that Doubleday gave baseball its identity.

The commission said Doubleday walked off the base paths to form a diamond and wrote down most of the basic rules. As of 2012, no public records from 1839 or 1840 have been discovered to confirm the commission's findings.

## Early Teams, Early Titles

The New York Knickerbockers were founded in 1845 as a social club. They are considered baseball's first team. Alexander Cartwright was the club's leader. The group established some early playing rules. One such rule was that outs could be made when a fielder struck a base runner with a thrown ball. Of course, that kickball-like rule did not last long.

On June 19, 1846, the Knickerbockers and the New York Baseball Club competed in the first organized contest. Amateur baseball in America continued to evolve over the next three decades. Along with 15 other teams, the Knickerbockers in 1857 formed the National Association of Base Ball Players (NABBP). It was the sport's first governing body. The NABBP also created a league championship.

Baseball saw a surge of popularity among soldiers during the Civil War, which lasted from 1861 to 1865. They developed universal rules during that time. Two years after the Civil War ended, more than 400 amateur clubs were competing across the country.

In 1871, the National Association of Professional Base Ball Players (NAPBBP) was founded. It is recognized as the first professional league. The NAPBBP absorbed several teams from the NABBP and lasted through the 1875 season. Some current NL teams can trace their roots to these clubs.

The current NL was formed on February 2, 1876. The first pitch of the NL's first game occurred on April 22 of that year, at Jefferson State Grounds in Philadelphia. The Boston Red Stockings beat the Philadelphia Athletics, 6–5.

Over the next 22 years, the NL competed against various short-lived leagues. Among them were the American Association (AA), the Union Association, and the Players League. Different versions of league championships were played. However, most were disorganized and did not last.

One such series was the "Championship of the United States." It was first played in 1884. The NL's Providence Grays faced the AA's New York Metropolitans Club. When the Grays emerged victorious, newspapers declared the club "World Champions." The term is still used today.

After the 1891 season, the AA ceased operations. The championship series was suspended, too. The NL expanded to 12 teams for the next season. It then split the season in two. The winner from the season's first half would face the winner of the second half for the championship. But the format failed to generate fan interest.

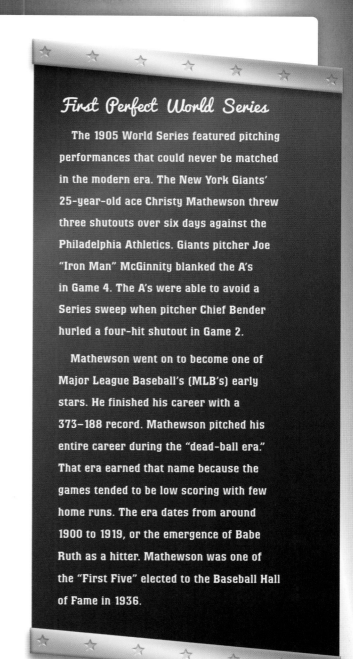

## First Perfect World Series

The 1905 World Series featured pitching performances that could never be matched in the modern era. The New York Giants' 25-year-old ace Christy Mathewson threw three shutouts over six days against the Philadelphia Athletics. Giants pitcher Joe "Iron Man" McGinnity blanked the A's in Game 4. The A's were able to avoid a Series sweep when pitcher Chief Bender hurled a four-hit shutout in Game 2.

Mathewson went on to become one of Major League Baseball's (MLB's) early stars. He finished his career with a 373–188 record. Mathewson pitched his entire career during the "dead-ball era." That era earned that name because the games tended to be low scoring with few home runs. The era dates from around 1900 to 1919, or the emergence of Babe Ruth as a hitter. Mathewson was one of the "First Five" elected to the Baseball Hall of Fame in 1936.

## An Odd Rule

The first World Series was played with an unusual rule. There were overflow crowds at Pittsburgh's Exposition Park. The park featured ropes, rather than fences, to keep fans off the field. So if a batter struck a ball and it rolled under an outfield rope into the area where fans were standing, it was deemed a ground-rule triple. In the four games at the park, 17 ground-rule triples were called.

Next up was the "Temple Cup" in 1894. This format pitted the first- and second-place clubs in the seven-game Cup finals. Only four Temple Cup winners were crowned.

## The World Series at Last

The NL was the only established major league at the turn of the twentieth century. So in 1901, the AL formed to challenge the NL. People from the two leagues did not initially get along. But two years later they agreed to try a new championship format. In 1903, the AL champion and the NL champion met in a nine-game series to determine the overall champion. The championship was called the World Series.

The AL's Boston Americans and the NL's Pittsburgh Pirates met in the first Fall Classic. On October 1, 1903, they played the first World Series game. Pitcher Cy Young started for the Americans. Young, the staff ace,

Fans roam the field at Huntington Avenue Baseball Grounds in Boston after the Pittsburgh Pirates beat the Boston Americans 7–3 in Game 1 of the 1903 World Series.

finished his career with a record 511 wins. Today, the Cy Young Award is given to the best pitcher in both the AL and the NL each season.

However, Young had a tough Game 1 against the Pirates. He gave up four first-inning runs and became the first pitcher to lose a World Series game. But Young rebounded. He earned wins in Games 5 and 7. The Americans captured the first World Series in an upset, five games to three.

The next season, the NL champion New York Giants boycotted the World Series. Their manager, John McGraw, did not believe the defending-champion Americans were worthy. The World Series resumed in 1905, though. This time it was here to stay.

**CHASING PENNANTS**

# The Yankees Dynasty

I t was a cold winter's day in 1920 when Boston Red Sox owner Harry Frazee formally announced the deal. On December 26, 1919, Frazee had sold the rights to outfielder George Herman "Babe" Ruth to the New York Yankees for $125,000 and considerations.

The Red Sox were baseball's dominant team of that era. They had won four World Series titles from 1912 to 1918. Ruth was a young pitcher in the 1915 and 1916 World Series triumphs. In 1918 he was a star. He pitched a complete-game shutout in the opener and also won Game 4. At one

Babe Ruth helped the Boston Red Sox win three World Series as a pitcher before being sold to the New York Yankees in 1920 and becoming an outfielder.

point he pitched 29 2/3 consecutive scoreless World Series innings for the Red Sox.

However, Ruth was beginning a transition from pitcher to outfielder. In 1919, the 24-year-old Ruth made the switch full time. That year he hit 29 home runs. No other major leaguer that year hit more than 12. He appeared to be on a track to superstardom.

There are different theories as to why Frazee sold Ruth before that 1920 season. Some believe he was trying to raise money for other business ventures. The most common explanation is that Ruth simply demanded too high a salary. Either way, he proved to be worth every penny to the Yankees.

## The Rise of the Yankees

The New York Yankees began in 1901 as the Baltimore Orioles. They moved to New York in 1903 and became the Highlanders. Then they changed their name to the Yankees in 1913. Through 1920, however, the team had never appeared in a World Series.

After Ruth's arrival, the Yankees appeared in 29 World Series from 1920 to 1964. They won 20 of those Fall Classics. Though Ruth played only in the first seven of those World Series, his arrival is usually considered when the Yankees dynasty began. His former team, meanwhile, did not

## Cubs Curse

In 1945, the Chicago Cubs were playing the Detroit Tigers in the World Series. Billy Sianis owned the Billy Goat Tavern in Chicago. He attended Game 4 along with his pet goat. However, the goat's odor upset some fans. Sianis was asked to leave. As he did, Sianis reportedly cursed the Cubs, who had won the World Series in 1907 and 1908, from ever winning another Fall Classic. When Sianis and his pet were ejected, the Cubs were leading the series two games to one. They ended up losing in seven games. They have not won another World Series through 2012.

win another World Series until 2004. The drought became know as the "Curse of the Bambino," named for Ruth's nickname.

In Ruth's first two seasons with the Yankees, he set records with 54 and 59 homers, respectively. That officially ended the dead-ball era. Before he was done, the Yankees were well on their way to being the most successful baseball team ever. And Ruth earned his place as arguably the greatest baseball player of all time.

## Murderers' Row

Ruth and the Yankees lost two World Series in 1921 and 1922. They finally overcame the New York Giants in 1923 to win their first World Series. Many considered the 1926 team to be the best yet.

New York Yankees first baseman Lou Gehrig hits the ball into the outfield during the 1927 World Series against the Pittsburgh Pirates.

The Yankees' batting lineup that year featured Ruth, first baseman Lou Gehrig, and outfielder Earle Combs. It became known as "Murderers' Row" for its tremendous offensive output. New York was heavily favored against the St. Louis Cardinals in the World Series that year. Ruth clubbed three home runs in Game 4.

However, Ruth was not perfect. In Game 7, the Yankees trailed 3–2 in the ninth inning. Ruth had hit a home run earlier. In the ninth he drew a walk. It was his eleventh walk of the World Series. New York's Bob Meusel stepped in the box to keep the rally going. But the cleanup batter never got a chance. Ruth was caught stealing second base to end the World Series.

Ruth more than made up for it the next year, though. The 1927 Yankees might have been the greatest baseball team of all time. Ruth, Gehrig, and Combs led the team to 110 regular-season wins. Then they swept the Pittsburgh Pirates in four games in the World Series. The 1928 Yankees were not quite as dominant, but they were close. They won 101 games before sweeping the Cardinals in the World Series.

Ruth and Gehrig won one more World Series together. They swept the Chicago Cubs in 1932. Ruth was 37 by then and had just two more seasons left in New York. But his 15 seasons there helped establish the Yankees as baseball's bona fide power.

"The Bambino" appeared in 10 World Series during his long career. In 41 career World Series games, he hit .326 with 15 homers and 33 RBIs. Ruth also went 3–0 with an 0.87 earned-run average (ERA) as a pitcher with the Red Sox.

## New York, New York

New York was at the center of the baseball universe from 1947 to 1964. During that time, at least one of the Yankees, the New York Giants, or the Brooklyn Dodgers played in 16 of the 18 World Series. Between 1921 and 1956, 13 World Series featured two New York teams.

In 1954, the Giants won their only World Series of the era. That year, a young outfielder named Willie Mays led the team past the Cleveland Indians in a four-game sweep. It was the only World Series win in four attempts during Mays's Hall of Fame career.

The next year it was the Dodgers' turn. For years, Brooklyn had been known as a good team that could not quite win the big one. Since the first World Series in 1903, the Dodgers had won seven NL pennants. Yet they had never won in the Fall Classic. Five of those losses had come against the Yankees. That finally changed in 1955, in the first World Series to be broadcast on color television.

## "The Catch"

The New York Giants and the Cleveland Indians were tied 2–2 in the eighth inning of the first game of the 1954 World Series. Cleveland had runners on first and second. First baseman Vic Wertz came to bat and ripped a liner nearly 460 feet (140.2 m) from home plate. Surely the two runs would score. Giants center fielder Willie Mays made sure they did not. He raced to deep center at the massive Polo Grounds. With his back to the infield, Mays reached out and made an over-the-shoulder catch. The Giants went on to win the series in four games. The play has become known simply as "The Catch."

New York Giants outfielder Willie Mays runs with his back to the infield to make "The Catch" against the Cleveland Indians during Game 1 of the 1954 World Series.

Dodgers pitcher Johnny Podres earned a complete-game victory in Game 3 on his twenty-third birthday. That helped bring Brooklyn back into the series after losing the first two games. Then Podres tossed a complete-game shutout in Game 7. The Dodgers won 2–0 and finally claimed a championship. Podres, meanwhile, was named the first World Series MVP.

The 1956 World Series was a rematch. This time, with the series tied at 2–2, Yankees pitcher Don Larsen faced 27 batters and retired all 27. Through 2012 no other pitcher had pitched a perfect game or no-hitter in the World Series. The Yankees ended up winning the series in seven games.

**THE YANKEES DYNASTY**

## Maz's Shot

The 1960 World Series featured two star-studded teams in the New York Yankees and Pittsburgh Pirates. Pittsburgh had not been to the World Series since 1927. The Yankees were appearing in their tenth World Series in 12 years. New York outscored the Pirates 55–27 in the series. Yankees ace pitcher Whitey Ford recorded two complete-game shutouts. Yet the Yankees still lost the series.

Bill Mazeroski was known throughout his 17-year career as a slick-fielding second baseman. He won eight Gold Gloves. Yet he became forever known for his bat. In Game 7, he hit a walk-off, series-clinching home run. Through 2012, the blast remained the only Game 7 walk-off homer in World Series history. The Pirates won 10–9 to take the World Series title.

Unsung Yankees second baseman Bobby Richardson hit .367 and drove in a record 12 runs. He was the lone World Series MVP from a losing squad through 2012.

## Another Yankees Dynasty

After the 1957 season, the Dodgers moved to Los Angeles and the Giants moved to San Francisco. That left the Yankees as the only team remaining in New York until 1962. In a way, that was fitting. Though the Dodgers and Giants had success, no team in baseball history could match the Yankees from 1947 to 1964. There were 18 World Series during those years. The Yankees appeared in 15 Fall Classics and won 10 of them.

At the center of those teams were outfielders Joe DiMaggio and Mickey Mantle. DiMaggio served in the military

## Sweet Sandy

The Dodgers and New York Yankees met in the World Series seven times prior to the 1963 edition. This matchup was different. It was the first time the longtime, cross-city rivals met at Yankee Stadium since the Dodgers relocated from Brooklyn to Los Angeles in 1958. In the Dodgers' return visit to New York, pitcher Sandy Koufax made them feel right at home. The left-hander was considered one of the decade's top pitchers. He proved it in Game 1. The Series MVP struck out a then-record 15 Yankees during a 5–2 victory.

during World War II and missed the 1943, 1944, and 1945 seasons. Besides that, he led the Yankees from 1936 to 1951. "The Yankee Clipper" won nine World Series in his 13 seasons.

The 1951 season was DiMaggio's last and Mantle's first. It was also the third in a string of five straight World Series titles for the Yankees. No team had matched that through 2012.

Mantle became a regular starter at age 20 in 1952. The Yankees won seven World Series during his 18 seasons. Other stars certainly helped. Ace pitcher Whitey Ford hurled for the Yankees in 1950 and again from 1953 to 1967. Slugging outfielder Roger Maris teamed with Mantle to make the "M&M Boys" combo from 1960 to 1966.

However, it was catcher Yogi Berra who went down as the winningest player in World Series history. Between 1946 and 1963, he appeared in a record 14 World Series and won 10. Through 2012, no player had surpassed Berra's 75 games, 259 at-bats, 71 hits, 10 doubles, or 49 singles in the World Series.

"How quickly can the Yankees come back?" a *New York Times* article asked in 1966, as the Yankees struggled to a last-place finish. "The answer is: Never. Not to what they were. Not to the level that symbolized perpetual success, power, and wealth. Not to that monopoly of victory which brought them five pennants in a row twice, four in a row two other times, and three straight three times. . . . It is no longer possible for any baseball team to achieve such superiority, and it never will be again."

New York Yankees catcher Yogi Berra tags Philadelphia Phillies shortstop Granny Hamner for an out during Game 4 of the 1950 World Series.

THE WORLD SERIES

# A Thrilling Era

Starting his wind-up, St. Louis Cardinals ace Bob Gibson often paused with his arms straightened over his head. Then, like lightning, Gibson would uncoil and release his pitch. It was often his high-rising fastball. To batters who faced Gibson in the 1964, 1967, and 1968 World Series, it was an intimidating prospect.

The Cardinals had won six World Series, beginning in 1926. However, that era clearly belonged to the New York Yankees. That team had won 20

St. Louis Cardinals ace Bob Gibson winds up to deliver a pitch to a Detroit Tigers hitter in the 1968 World Series.

## Tiger Time

Talk about coming through in the clutch. Detroit Tigers pitcher Mickey Lolich did just that in the 1968 World Series. He pitched three complete-game wins to lift the Tigers over the St. Louis Cardinals in seven games. On two-days' rest, Lolich outdueled Cardinals ace Bob Gibson in the deciding contest. Lolich (3–0) was named World Series MVP. In 27 innings, he gave up five runs and struck out 21. The 1968 season was tabbed "The Year of the Pitcher."

The Cardinals had jumped out to a 3–1 series lead. The momentum seemed to change with one play in Game 5. Tigers catcher Bill Freehan tagged out Cardinals speedster Lou Brock during a home-plate collision. Brock was one of the best base runners ever. Many fans still question why Brock elected to go in standing and not slide on the play.

World Series between 1920 and 1964. Gibson effectively put an end to the Yankees' dynasty in 1964.

The right-handed flamethrower highlighted the time of the overpowering pitcher. The Yankees and Cardinals split the first four games of the 1964 World Series. In Game 5, Gibson gave up a two-run homer to Tom Tresh in the bottom of the ninth inning. It tied the game. But Gibson did not give up. He returned to the mound for the 10th inning and held the Yankees scoreless as the Cardinals won 5–2.

The Yankees came back to tie the series in Game 6. On short rest, Gibson returned to the mound for Game 7.

He pitched a complete game as St. Louis won 7–5. Gibson struck out 31 batters in 27 innings with a 3.00 ERA during the World Series to earn the MVP Award. That proved to be the Yankees' last World Series appearance until 1976.

Gibson and the Cardinals were just beginning. In 1967, Gibson pitched three complete-game victories against the "Impossible Dream" Boston Red Sox. The name came because few expected the Red Sox could win the pennant that year. They would not win the World Series though. In the three wins, Gibson surrendered just three runs and struck out 26 batters. Gibson, who missed parts of the regular season with a broken leg,

## Miracle Mets

Some call them the "Miracle Mets." Others refer to them as the "Amazin' Mets." Whatever anyone says about the 1969 New York Mets, their World Series championship was truly incredible. In their previous seven seasons, the Mets had never finished better than ninth place. Before 1969, the NL was a single 10-team league. In 1969, they reached the World Series against the Baltimore Orioles. After dropping Game 1, the Mets won four consecutive games to claim one of the greatest upsets in baseball history. Mets first baseman Donn Clendenon hit .357 and clubbed three home runs to earn the World Series MVP Award.

even clubbed a Game 7 home run to cement his second World Series MVP Award. In his first two World Series, Gibson had a 2.00 ERA.

The Cardinals were back in the World Series the next year. And Gibson was once again brilliant. He tossed three complete games against the Detroit Tigers. In Game 1, Gibson struck out a World Series-record 17 batters. Through 2012, the record had yet to be broken. However, the Tigers beat the Cardinals in seven games.

## Waving it Fair

The Red Sox, denied by the Cardinals in 1967, were back in the World Series in 1975. And in the bottom of the 12th in Game 6, Red Sox catcher Carlton Fisk stood near home plate waving. If Fisk's hit stayed fair, it would be a home run and the Red Sox would survive until Game 7. So he waved, trying to will it to go over the outfield wall in fair territory.

The ball ended up hitting the left-field foul pole. That meant it was not only fair—it was a home run. Fisk erupted in celebration. Many call Fisk's walk-off homer one of the greatest World Series moments ever. Many call Game 6 between the Red Sox and Cincinnati Reds one of the greatest World Series contests ever played.

It certainly was worth the wait. Because of rain, Game 6 was played five nights after Game 5. The excitement started early. Boston's star rookie outfielder Fred Lynn slammed a two-out, three-run homer in the third.

Carlton Fisk of the Boston Red Sox attempts to will his 12th-inning home run fair during Game 6 of the 1975 World Series against the Cincinnati Reds.

However, Cincinnati answered in the fifth. Outfielder Ken Griffey drove in two runs on a triple. Then catcher Johnny Bench singled to score Griffey.

The Reds built a 6–3 lead going into the bottom of the eighth. The Reds, already ahead three games to two, appeared on their way to the World Series title. But Boston came back.

Lynn led off with a single. Teammate Rico Petrocelli drew a walk. The next two Red Sox got out. Then Bernie Carbo stepped to the plate. He looked bad, then great, during the at-bat. On a 2–2 pitch, Carbo was fooled as he awkwardly fouled off a pitch. His next swing was better.

## Mr. October

Reggie Jackson was a Hall of Fame slugger best known for his dramatic World Series home runs and off-field dramatics. Jackson helped the Oakland Athletics dominate baseball during the first half of the 1970s. The A's captured three consecutive World Series titles from 1972 to 1974. He later won two more World Series with the New York Yankees in 1977 and 1978. Jackson was one of the first major leaguers in many years to wear facial hair. He appeared at 1972 spring training with a full mustache. Soon most of Jackson's teammates grew mustaches of their own. Jackson ended his 21-year career with 563 homers and 1,702 RBI. In 27 World Series games, "Mr. October" slammed 10 homers. Three of those came in Game 6 of the 1977 World Series.

He drilled a game-tying, three-run homer to center field.

The Red Sox nearly won in the bottom of the ninth. Lynn hit a short fly ball. George Foster grabbed it for the out and instantly threw home. Base runner Denny Doyle thought he heard the third-base coach scream "Go . . . go . . . go!" So Doyle ran toward home plate. But the coach was actually yelling "No . . . no . . . no!" Doyle was tagged out at home.

Neither team scored in the 10th inning. It appeared that Reds second baseman Joe Morgan connected on a two-run home run in the 12th. But Red Sox right fielder Dwight Evans raced to catch what would have otherwise been a home run. Reds manager Sparky Anderson later said Evans's catch was one of the best he'd witnessed in World Series history.

Will McEnaney (37), Johnny Bench (5), and Pete Rose (14) celebrate after the Cincinnati Reds beat the Boston Red Sox in Game 7 of the 1975 World Series.

Finally, in the bottom of the 12th, Fisk "waved" his home run fair and the Red Sox won 7–6. However, the "Curse of the Bambino" was still in effect. Cincinnati won 4–3 to take the series in Game 7. One year later, the Reds and their dominant "Big Red Machine" lineup swept the Yankees to claim another World Series title.

Behind outfielder Reggie "Mr. October" Jackson, the Yankees came back to win the next two World Series, in 1977 and 1978. That made them the third team in a row to win consecutive World Series. In fact, the Oakland Athletics had won three in a row from 1972 to 1974. It was not until 1992 and 1993 that another team won back-to-back titles.

# Amazing Moments

Red Sox veteran Bill Buckner positioned himself at first base. He readied himself for closer Bob Stanley's full-count pitch. Outfielder Mookie Wilson of the New York Mets swung at the pitch. He sent the ball rolling slowly up the first-base line. It looked like a routine play for Buckner. But it was not.

The ball bounced between Buckner's legs and into right field. Mets base runner Ray Knight raced toward home. He leapt and landed on the plate, giving the Mets a 6–5 win.

The ball rolls past Boston Red Sox first baseman Bill Buckner in the bottom of the 10th inning of Game 6 of the 1986 World Series.

What a turn of events. If Red Sox fans did not believe in the "Curse of the Bambino" before the 10th inning of Game 6 of the 1986 World Series, many did soon after.

The Red Sox had twice been one strike away from clinching their first Fall Classic since 1918. They came into the bottom of the 10th with a 5–3 lead. Then with two outs and two strikes, Mets third baseman Knight hit an RBI single to cut the lead by one. Wilson was up next. He had two strikes when a wild pitch allowed the Mets to tie the game at 5–5. Finally, Buckner's famous error allowed the Mets to win a wild Game 6 and force a Game 7.

The teams had to wait a night because of rain. The extra time appeared to be exactly what the Red Sox needed. Outfielder Dwight Evans and catcher Rich Gedman hit back-to-back home runs in the second to put Boston up 2–0. The Red Sox added another run later that inning. But Knight and outfielder Darryl Strawberry answered with home runs for the Mets. That duo powered the Mets to an 8–5 victory. It sealed their second World Series title after first winning in 1969.

Buckner's error and all the World Series drama only served to punctuate one of the most dramatic postseasons in baseball history. The California Angels had jumped out to a 3–1 series lead in the ALCS before Boston came back to win. In the NLCS, a 16-inning masterpiece highlighted the Mets' series win over the Houston Astros.

## Hobbled Gibby

Kirk Gibson was injured. He was barely able to stand, let alone run. Yet the Los Angeles Dodgers' outfielder attempted to stay loose, just in case.

### Earthquake

A large earthquake shook the Bay Area of Northern California just before Game 3 of the 1989 World Series was scheduled to begin. The series between the San Francisco Giants and the Oakland Athletics was postponed for 10 days. However, the Athletics came back to sweep their neighbors in four games.

Kirk Gibson of the Los Angeles Dodgers rounds third base after his pinch-hit home run in the bottom of the ninth in Game 1 of the 1988 World Series.

He took practice swings in the Dodgers' clubhouse. His loud, agonizing grunts could be heard outside the door. It was a good thing he was warming up. It turned out the Dodgers would need him.

The Dodgers trailed the Oakland Athletics 4–3 in the bottom of the ninth in Game 1 of the 1988 World Series. Oakland's dominant closer Dennis Eckersley issued a walk to pinch-hitter Mike Davis. Then Dodgers manager Tommy Lasorda summoned Gibson.

Gibson hobbled up to the batter's box. He was known as a power hitter. However, his swings looked uneven as he fouled off a few pitches. Gibson tried to run to first after tapping a soft grounder down the first-base line. He limped back after it went foul. Two pitches later, Gibson made contact again. This time he drilled a slider into the right field seats for a walk-off home run.

Gibson pumped his fists wildly as he hobbled around the bases. He had become the first batter to end a World Series game on a come-from-behind home run. And he did it in his only at-bat during the series. Dodgers ace Orel Hershiser went on to win Games 2 and 5. He struck out 17 batters in 16 innings to earn MVP honors. The Dodgers captured the series four games to one.

## Twins outlast Braves

Before 1991, no team had ever risen from last place the previous season to a league pennant. In 1991, both the Minnesota Twins and the Atlanta Braves accomplished the feat.

The unlikely opponents played a total of 69 innings to decide the championship. It remained the longest seven-game series in history through 2012. Five of the seven games were decided by one run. Four games were won on a team's final at-bat. Three games went into extra innings. When it was done, many called it the best ever.

## Blue Jays Fly High

Winning consecutive World Series titles became increasingly difficult as baseball expanded. But the Toronto Blue Jays did just that in 1992 and 1993. Their 1992 victory over the Atlanta Braves marked the first time the Commissioner's Trophy was awarded to a non-US team. Blue Jays catcher Pat Borders hit .450 to become one of the most unlikely World Series MVPs.

Toronto faced the Philadelphia Phillies in the 1993 Fall Classic. Slugging outfielder Joe Carter clinched the series with a three-run, walk-off home run in Game 6. He joined the Pittsburgh Pirates' Bill Mazeroski (1960) as the lone players to seal a World Series with a walk-off homer in the bottom of the ninth inning.

Blue Jays designated hitter Paul Molitor earned MVP honors. Molitor hit .500 with two homers and eight RBIs. Molitor was a full-time designated hitter, but he was called upon to make a rare start at first base in Game 3.

The Twins opened the series with two wins at home. Then the teams went to Atlanta for three games. It was past midnight when Game 3 went into the bottom of the 12th inning. The timing was perfect for Braves second baseman Mark Lemke. Braves outfielder David Justice started the winning rally with a single. He then stole second and scored on Lemke's two-out hit. Lemke came through again in the bottom of the ninth of Game 4. The game was tied 2–2. Then Lemke tripled and scored on a controversial hook slide past Twins catcher Brian Harper. The Braves appeared to gain the series momentum after routing the Twins 14–5 in Game 5.

## Series Strikes Out

A players' strike in August 1994 forced the cancellation of the 1994 World Series. It was the first time the Fall Classic was not played since 1904. The World Series resumed in 1995. It proved to be a tight matchup between the Atlanta Braves and the Cleveland Indians. The Braves clinched the championship, four games to two. Five outcomes were decided by one run. Braves pitchers Tom Glavine and Mark Wohlers combined on a one-hitter to win Game 6 by a score of 1–0. The Braves also became the first team to capture World Series titles in three cities. The Boston Braves won in 1914 and the Milwaukee Braves in 1957.

As it turned out, the series was just starting to become interesting. Game 6 was back in Minnesota. And this one belonged to star center fielder Kirby Puckett. "You guys should jump on my back tonight," he told his teammates before the game. "I'm going to carry us."

And that is what he did. Puckett opened the game with an RBI triple in the first inning. In the third, the 5-foot-8 Puckett leaped against the left-center fence to rob an extra-base hit. Then he hit a sacrifice fly to drive in another run in the fifth.

His biggest moment, however, came in the bottom of the 11th inning. The game was tied 3–3. Puckett took two balls and a strike to get a feel for Braves pitcher Charlie Leibrandt. Then Puckett launched a walk-off home run over the center-field wall.

"And we'll see you tomorrow night!" CBS sportscaster Jack Buck announced to the national audience. The Metrodome in Minneapolis sounded like a "plane taking off on the runway," one teammate recalled. The moment of Puckett rounding the bases and pumping his fist was captured in a statue outside the Twins' new ballpark.

Game 7 the next night was an appropriate conclusion to the wild series. It ended up being a pitching duel for the ages: Jack Morris versus John Smoltz. After nine innings, the score remained 0–0. The 24-year-old Smoltz had blanked the Twins through 7 1/3 innings before the Braves went to the bullpen. The 36-year-old Morris came back for more in the 10th. And once again, he kept the Braves off the board. After 10 innings, Morris had thrown 126 pitches. He had allowed seven hits with eight strikeouts and two walks. He did not need to come back out.

Twins pinch hitter Gene Larkin singled home outfielder Dan Gladden with the World Series-clinching run in the bottom of the 10th inning. In his three World Series starts, Morris pitched a combined 23 innings and allowed just three runs. Morris was named World Series MVP after one of the most remarkable Fall Classics.

Minnesota Twins outfielder Kirby Puckett celebrates as he rounds the bases after his walk-off home run in Game 6 of the 1991 World Series.

# Chapter 6

# Fall Classics Continue

**N**ew York Yankees shortstop Derek Jeter was just a 22-year-old rookie in 1996. He could have had no idea what his career would hold. It had been decades since the dynasties of Babe Ruth and Lou Gehrig, of Joe DiMaggio, and of Mickey Mantle. The Yankees had not even been to the World Series since 1981. Jeter would soon lead the Bronx Bombers to a new era of success. And by the end of his career, Jeter would join Ruth, Gehrig, DiMaggio, Mantle, and Yogi Berra as Yankees legends who brought multiple World Series to New York.

New York Yankees shortstop Derek Jeter reacts after his team defeated the New York Mets 3–2 in Game 4 of the 2000 World Series.

## Pitching Duo Power

The Arizona Diamondbacks in 2001 stopped the New York Yankees from winning a fifth World Series in six seasons. And Arizona did it with a powerful 1–2 pitching punch. Starters Randy Johnson and Curt Schilling were named co-MVPs of the World Series. The duo combined for a 4–0 record with a 1.40 ERA and 45 strikeouts in 39 1/3 innings.

Still, the World Series came down to a thrilling Game 7. The Yankees' legendary closer Mariano Rivera was pitching with a 2–1 lead in the bottom of the ninth inning. However, he gave up one run on shortstop Tony Womack's double with one out. Then Diamondbacks outfielder Luis Gonzalez singled in teammate Jay Bell for the 3–2 victory.

The Diamondbacks had only begun as a team in 1998. They also became the first western team outside of California to win a World Series.

## Four in Five

The Atlanta Braves opened the 1996 World Series by outscoring the Yankees 16–1 in two wins. But the Braves could not finish what they started. The NL champs batted .315 during the opening six innings of games. That average slipped to .176 in the later innings. The Yankees had fewer homers, runs, hits, and a higher team ERA. Yet they rallied to win the final four games.

The World Series win was the Yankees' first since 1978. The wait for more was short. They won three in a row from 1998 to 2000. They beat the San Diego Padres, the Braves, and then the New York Mets.

## Marlins Magic

The Florida (later Miami) Marlins demonstrated a flair for the dramatic in their 1997 and 2003 World Series championships. During their first appearance, the Marlins trailed the Cleveland Indians by a run in the bottom of the ninth inning of Game 7. The Marlins tied the game in the ninth. Then shortstop Edgar Renteria drove home teammate Craig Counsell with the series-clinching run in the 11th off a soft line drive that skimmed the glove of pitcher Charles Nagy. In 2003 the Marlins upset the New York Yankees in six games. The Marlins triumphed despite being outscored 21–17.

The Yankees also won the AL pennant in 2001 and 2003 before winning another World Series in 2009.

Several key players took part in those World Series victories. Four were there for the entire run: Jeter, catcher Jorge Posada, starting pitcher Andy Pettitte, and bat-breaking closer Mariano Rivera.

Perhaps the most memorable World Series win during that era was the "Subway Series" in 2000 between the Yankees and Mets. For the first time since 1956, both World Series teams were from New York.

Game 1 in 2000 was a marathon. It lasted 4 hours, 51 minutes. The Yankees finally put away the Mets thanks to Jose Vizcaino, a career reserve infielder. He drove home first baseman Tino Martinez with the winning run in the 12th inning.

The Yankees extended their World Series winning streak to 14 games with a Game 2 victory. The Mets climbed back to win Game 3. But their momentum seemed to end after Jeter's leadoff home run in Game 4. Jeter also homered in the clinching Game 5 and was named World Series MVP.

Jeter won his fifth World Series in 2009 over the Philadelphia Phillies. The Yankees won 7–3 in Game 6 to take the series. Designated hitter Hideki Matsui was the star. He drove in six of those runs for New York. Through 2011, only two other players (the Yankees' Bobby Richardson in 1960 and the St. Louis Cardinals' Albert Pujols in 2011) had driven in that many runs in a World Series game.

## Breaking The Curse

The Boston Red Sox traded Babe Ruth to the Yankees in 1920. Through 2004, the Yankees had won 26 World Series. The Red Sox, meanwhile, had won none, although they had reached the World Series four times. After 86 years, the "Curse of the Bambino" finally ended in 2004.

The amazing run began in the ALCS between the Red Sox and Yankees. New York won the first three games. That included a 19–8 drubbing in Game 3. Then Boston became the first team ever to come back from three games down to win a postseason series.

David Ortiz of the Boston Red Sox blasts a three-run home run in the first inning of Game 1 of the 2004 World Series against the St. Louis Cardinals.

After that, there was no way the Cardinals could stop the Red Sox in the World Series. Behind ace Curt Schilling and sluggers such as designated hitter David Ortiz and outfielder Manny Ramirez, Boston swept St. Louis in four games. Ramirez was named the World Series MVP after hitting .412 and driving in four runs.

"This is for anyone who ever played for the Red Sox, anyone who ever rooted for the Red Sox, anyone who ever saw a game at Fenway Park," Red Sox General Manager Theo Epstein said. "This is bigger than the 25 guys in this clubhouse. This is for all of Red Sox Nation, past and present."

Three years later, Boston returned to the Fall Classic. This time the Red Sox swept the Colorado Rockies in four games. The "Curse of the Bambino" was officially over.

FALL CLASSICS CONTINUE

## Chicago Success

The Chicago Cubs "Curse of the Billygoat" gets a lot of attention. Going into the 2005 World Series, however, the Chicago White Sox had a similarly long drought. Their last pennant had been in 1959. Their last World Series win was in 1917. The Cubs had not been to the Fall Classic since 1945 or won since 1908. However, the White Sox ended their drought in 2005 with a four-game sweep over the Houston Astros.

## Old and New

Baseball is a game of traditions and history. Between 2001 and 2012, some of baseball's most storied teams won World Series titles. Behind their captain Jeter, the Yankees won their twenty-seventh Fall Classic in 2009. Pujols led his Cardinals to their tenth and eleventh World Series in 2006 and 2011. Through 2011, no teams have more World Series victories than the Yankees and Cardinals.

Some other classic teams ended long winning droughts during that era. In 2008, the Philadelphia Phillies won their second World Series in their 125 years of existence. Two years later, a quirky but effective pitching staff led the Giants to their first World Series since moving to San Francisco from New York in 1958. Then they won another in 2012.

Catcher Carlos Ruiz runs to celebrate with pitcher Brad Lidge in 2008 after the Philadelphia Phillies claimed their first World Series title since 1980.

Yet the World Series also showcased a new era during that time. In 2001, the Arizona Diamondbacks won the World Series in just their fourth season. Two years later, the Florida Marlins won their second World Series title in their first 11 years as a team. The Rockies and Tampa Bay Rays only came in to the major leagues in 1993 and 1998, respectively. Yet in 2007 (Colorado) and 2008 (Tampa Bay) they each reached the World Series for the first time.

The World Series has been a fall tradition for more than a century. It has been held every year but two since 1903. Each era has brought its own stars and rivalries. But one thing has always remained the same: The World Series has lived up to its name as the Fall Classic.

# TIMELINE

The first baseball team, the New York Knickerbockers, begins play as a social club.
**1845**

The Philadelphia Athletics beat the Chicago White Stockings for the first NAPBBP pennant.
**1871**

The first World Series game is played between the AL's Boston Americans and NL's Pittsburgh Pirates. Boston wins the series.
**1903**

New York Giants outfielder Fred Snodgrass drops a routine pop-up in the 10th inning of Game 8 of the World Series. The error leads to the Red Sox claiming the title.
**1912**

Red Sox owner Harry Frazee announces he is selling outfielder Babe Ruth to the Yankees. The Red Sox would not win another World Series for 84 years.
**1920**

Los Angeles Dodgers pitcher Sandy Koufax strikes out a then–World Series record 15 Yankees during a 5–2 victory in Game 1.
**1963**

The St. Louis Cardinals' Bob Gibson pitches a complete-game 7–5 win over the Yankees in Game 7 of the World Series.
**1964**

Red Sox catcher Carlton Fisk waves his walk-off homer fair in the bottom of the 12th in Game 6 of the World Series. The Cincinnati Reds win Game 7.
**1975**

Yankees outfielder Reggie Jackson slams three home runs in Game 6 against the Dodgers in the first of back-to-back Yankees World Series titles.
**1977**

Red Sox first baseman Bill Buckner misplays a routine ground ball, allowing the New York Mets to win Game 6 of the World Series. The Mets also win Game 7.
**1986**

Ruth leads the Yankees to their first World Series title in six games over the New York Giants.

**1923**

With help from "The Catch," Hall of Famer Willie Mays leads the New York Giants to the World Series title.

**1954**

Brooklyn Dodgers pitcher Johnny Podres shuts out the Yankees in Game 7 of the World Series on October 4. It is the Dodgers' first title.

**1955**

Yankees pitcher Don Larsen pitches the only perfect game in World Series history on October 8.

**1956**

Pittsburgh Pirates second baseman Bill Mazeroski hits the first game-winning homer in Game 7 history against the Yankees on October 13.

**1960**

An earthquake shakes Northern California prior to the first pitch of Game 3 of the World Series. The Oakland Athletics eventually win after a 10-day break.

**1989**

Minnesota Twins pitcher Jack Morris throws a 10-inning, 1–0 shutout against the Atlanta Braves in Game 7 of the World Series.

**1991**

A players' strike results in the cancellation of part of the season and the World Series. It is only the second year without a World Series since 1903.

**1994**

The Red Sox complete a World Series sweep of the Cardinals. It is the Red Sox's first championship since 1918.

**2004**

Behind third baseman David Freese, the Cardinals win their eleventh World Series title in seven games over the Texas Rangers.

**2011**

## The Trophy

MLB formally introduced the Commissioner's Trophy to the winner of the World Series in 1967. Following each World Series, the commissioner of baseball presents the trophy to the winning team.

## The Legends

**Yogi Berra (New York Yankees):** The catcher won a record 10 World Series in a record 14 appearances from 1947 to 1963.

**Reggie Jackson (Oakland Athletics and New York Yankees):** "Mr. October" won five World Series from 1972 to 1978, though injuries kept him out of the 1972 Fall Classic.

**Don Larsen (New York Yankees):** The pitcher threw the only perfect game in World Series history in 1956. He also won in 1958.

**Jack Morris (Detroit Tigers, Minnesota Twins, Toronto Blue Jays):** The pitcher won three World Series on three different teams (1984, 1991, 1992).

## The Victors

**New York Yankees:** 27 championships

**St. Louis Cardinals:** 11

**Oakland (Philadelphia) Athletics:** 9

# GLOSSARY

**ace**
The best starting pitcher on a team's staff.

**amateur**
When an athlete is not allowed to be paid for competing.

**closer**
A pitcher who specializes in pitching the final inning of a game.

**drought**
A long period in which a team fails to do something, such as win a World Series.

**expansion**
Adding something new. In sports, new teams are called expansion teams.

**pennant**
A flag. In baseball, it symbolizes that a team has won its league championship.

**perfect game**
A game in which a pitcher retires every batter from the opposing team in order. In a nine-inning game, that means the pitcher faces 27 batters and gets them all out.

**walk-off**
A play that results in the game-ending run being scored.

**wild-card**
Playoff berths given to the best remaining teams that did not win their divisions.

## Selected Bibliography

Buckley, Jr., James. *Baseball*. New York: DK Publishing, 2000.

Buckley, Jr., James, and Jim Gigliotti. *Baseball A Celebration!* London; New York: DK Publishing, 2001.

Burns, Ken, and Geoffrey C. Ward. *Baseball: An Illustrated History*. New York: Alfred A. Knopf, 1994.

Robinson, Ray. *Greatest World Series Thrillers*. New York: Random House, 1965.

Vaccaro, Mike. *First Fall Classic*. New York: Doubleday, 2009.

Wong, Stephen. *Smithsonian Baseball*. New York: Smithsonian Books, 2005.

## Further Readings

Christopher, Matt. *The World Series: The Greatest Moments of the Most Exciting Games*. New York: Little Brown and Company, 2007.

Holub, Joan. *Who Was Babe Ruth?*. New York: Grosset & Dunlap, 2005.

James, Bill. *The New Bill James Historical Baseball Abstract*. New York: Simon & Schuster, 2001.

Kuenster, John. *The Best of Baseball Digest*. Chicago: Ivan R. Dee, 2006.

## Web Links

To learn more about the World Series, visit ABDO Publishing Company online at **www.abdopublishing.com**. Web sites about the World Series are featured on our Book Links page. These links are routinely monitored and updated to provide the most current information available.

## Places to Visit

**National Baseball Hall of Fame and Museum**
25 Main Street
Cooperstown, NY 13326
(888) HALL-OF-FAME
**www.baseballhall.org**
This hall of fame and museum highlights the greatest players and moments in the history of baseball. Among the World Series legends enshrined here are Yogi Berra, Bob Gibson, Willie Mays, and Babe Ruth.

**New York Yankees Museum presented by Bank of America**
1 East 161st Street
Bronx, NY 10451
(718) 293-4300
**http://newyork.yankees.mlb.com/nyy/ballpark/stadium_tours.jsp**
Located near Gate 6 at Yankee Stadium, this museum celebrates the history of the New York Yankees and their record 27 World Series wins.

# INDEX

## About the Author

Jeff Hawkins is a stay-at-home dad and an award-winning sportswriter. Career highlights include covering the NFL's Carolina Panthers (2011) and NHL's Chicago Blackhawks (2003–06). Hawkins spends most of his time writing and with his young son and wife at their North Carolina residence.